Rabén & Sjögren Stockholm

Translation copyright © 1991 by Barbara Lucas
All rights reserved
Pictures copyright © 1989 by Marit Törnqvist
Originally published in Sweden by Rabén & Sjögren under the title *När Bäckhultarn for till stan,*
text copyright © 1951 by Astrid Lindgren
Library of Congress catalog card number: 91-60168
Printed in Italy
First edition, 1991

ISBN 91 29 59920 2

R & S Books are distributed in the United States of America by Farrar, Straus and Giroux, New York;
in the United Kingdom by Ragged Bears, Andover; in Canada by Vanwell Publishing, St. Catharines;
and in Australia by ERA Publications, Adelaide

Astrid Lindgren

A Calf for Christmas

Pictures by Marit Törnqvist

Translated by Barbara Lucas

R&S
BOOKS

Stockholm   New York   London   Adelaide   Toronto

The snow fell and fell. When Johan came out on the front steps in the morning, he stood there a moment and just looked at it. The farm was almost buried in snow. And more kept coming — great, white flakes that fell silently and constantly.

It was so quiet — almost as if the whole world lay dead under a blanket of snow — the whole farm, the whole county, the whole of Sweden, the whole world!

Not truly dead, however. Somewhere far away, a sound was heard. It was the faint tinkling of sleigh bells coming nearer and growing stronger. Soon, Johan could see the sleigh down the road. It must be Peter Jonsson from Fairbrook driving to town.

When the sleigh had vanished from sight, Johan resolutely pushed his way through the drifts. He had to make a path down to the road, because he was going to school. It was the last day before the Christmas holidays. The snow came almost up to his waist. Down by the gatepost stood his kick-sled, though not much of it was visible. With some effort he pulled it loose and shook the snow off it.

Luckily, the road had been plowed, and it was downhill most of the way to school. He pumped hard to get up some speed. Then he stood on the runners and coasted down the first hill. As he steered through the snow flurries, he thought again about the awful thing. And then he suddenly had to screw up his eyes to keep the tears from streaming down his face.

The awful thing. It had happened yesterday. When Mom came out to the barn in the morning, she had found Emma dead in her stall. Completely dead. Emma had swallowed a nail, said the veterinarian who examined her afterward. Their only cow had eaten a nail and killed herself!

Johan's knuckles gripped hard on the kick-sled. It wasn't fair that such a thing should happen to someone poor who had only one cow. Peter Jonsson from Fairbrook had at least twenty cows, but had anyone ever heard of something so awful happening to any of them? Oh, no. They grew and thrived and were in quite good health, all of them. You could probably feed them foot-long nails without the slightest problem.

But his Emma! She was dead now. Completely dead. And she had been so alive . . . and so kind . . . and he had loved her so much. He thought about one especially nice evening last summer. He could recognize the smell of summer in his nose, just thinking about it. He had walked in the pasture for several hours, looking for Emma. She had to be milked, and it was Johan's job when he got home from school. But she had disappeared. He couldn't find her in any of her usual places. Finally, he became worried. Then suddenly he heard the little tinkling of her bell coming from Fairbrook's pasture. He called her and she burst noisily through the bushes, bellowing happily when she caught sight of him. The whole way to the milk stall, Johan fussed at her for making him so worried and for having broken through Peter Jonsson's fence. But when he sat down on the stool, with the milk bucket between his knees, and laid his head against her brown side, and the milk streamed in two thick rivulets through his hands, he couldn't be angry any longer. He could only love her.

But she was dead now. Completely dead. The barn stall was empty. He didn't have a cow anymore. And Mom had cried last night. That was almost worst of all. Johan had never seen her cry before. He didn't even know that she could. That she did so now made him realize just what a terrible misfortune it was, losing Emma. And Dad, who was always so cheerful and always knew what to do, had sat at the kitchen table and just sighed the whole evening.

There is no justice in the world, thought Johan. There is no help for those who are poor. Only dreadful things happen. The cow dies, and neither God nor anyone else cares. Johan pushed himself through the snow and suddenly felt very angry at God. He should be the one making sure that cows don't eat nails.

"But that doesn't happen, except maybe with Peter Jonsson's cows," said Johan aloud and bitterly. God certainly looked after them. He worried about them so much that he didn't have time to look after poor Emma.

He threw his sled aside, and with a heart full of bitterness and hands jammed savagely in his pockets, he stomped through the school gate.

Oh, so Peter Jonsson was in town today! That should liven things up. Partly because of the Christmas market and partly because ... well, partly because of Peter Jonsson. When he came to town, he came for a good time. And he had not driven ten miles in all that snow just to go around thirsty. A look of childlike anticipation spread over his face as he unharnessed his mare and handed her over to the innkeeper's stable.

Peter Jonsson was getting ready to have fun.

It was, by the way, a very smart mare he had, and that was a good thing for Peter Jonsson. Rose could find the way home all by herself if necessary. And it was necessary from time to time. Not often, but now and then. It might be necessary today. Because now Peter Jonsson entered the inn, rubbing his hands together cheerfully, and ordered a hearty breakfast.

All day, Rose stood in the stable and waited patiently for whatever would happen. In the late afternoon, she heard heavy clomping and rowdy laughing, so she knew that her master was ready to go home.

Yes, now Peter Jonsson did want to go home. He had a couple of men in tow who helped him harness Rose. It was a good thing, too, since just now Peter Jonsson certainly did not know which was the front and which was the back of a horse.

The men helped him climb into the front seat of the sleigh and stuck the reins into his hands. The rest they left up to Rose.

"But what about the calf?" shouted Peter Jonsson just as Rose was ready to set off. "Where is the calf?"

"Which calf?" said one of the men.

"My calf," said Peter Jonsson. "I just bought one over at Dram's farm. He was supposed to bring it here."

Peter Jonsson was right. There came Dram, carrying a little heifer calf which looked quite frightened.

With a lot of rowdy laughter and noisy jokes, they finally put the calf into a sack, which they tightened at the neck, so the calf wouldn't freeze. Only her head stuck out. The calf bellowed pitifully when they heaved her up on the sleigh. Peter Jonsson looked kindly at her and said, "Ah, little one, you'll be just fine there!"

Rose pawed the ground impatiently. She wanted to

get started. But first a bottle was passed around. Peter Jonsson got it last. He drank what was left and tossed the bottle away.

"Now I feel great," he said. Then he clucked at Rose to go, though that really wasn't necessary. She set off at a sharp trot through the gate. She wanted to go home.

She was not fond of town trips. They always ended in trouble. And as twilight fell, she trotted briskly to put the town behind her. Soon she was on the familiar road that led all the way home. As soon as they got there, she knew that her master would become himself again.

It had stopped snowing. One by one, the stars came out. But Peter Jonsson didn't notice. He slept. The reins hung slack in his hands. The only sound was the quiet tinkling of the sleigh bells. They did not disturb his sleep. And the sleigh's rhythmic movement rocked him all the more deeply into slumber. The forest was dark and still. The road turned and twisted, but Rose knew every crook, every stone on the roadside. Peter Jonsson could sleep peacefully.

Then a long drawn-out bellowing pierced the quiet darkness. Peter Jonsson sat up with a start. He looked around anxiously. What was that devilish sound?

There it was again! Good heavens! It was coming from the sleigh, his own sleigh! With great effort, he turned his head and looked behind him. And there it was, the monster. It lay, dimly visible in the starlight, staring at him with scary eyes. It was a head, nothing more. A scary head making scary noises. Wild with fright, Peter Jonsson grabbed the whip and snapped it over Rose's back. He knew what he had in the sleigh! The devil was lying there, shouting at him. He had heard about such things before, but that it should happen to him, a poor, ordinary sinner! He was being punished for his drinking. Oh, he would never touch a drop again.

He cracked the whip over Rose, and she ran as she had never run before. But again and again came the dreadful sound. Then Peter Jonsson became quite furious. After all, he was not obliged to chauffeur the devil around — indeed, he would not! Out of the sleigh the ugly thing would go, if it was the last thing Peter Jonsson ever did in his life.

He reined in Rose and staggered out of the sleigh.

"Now then, you wretched creature, you have ridden far enough!" he said.

Then came a new, horrifying bellow. But when Peter Jonsson was angry, he was really angry and nothing could scare him. Of course he didn't dare look at the miserable thing. He shut his eyes and groped around until he got hold of it and lifted it, heavy as it was, the scoundrel.

"But you won't break Peter Jonsson. Out of the sleigh you go, so help me God!

"There! Now it's done! Now you can lie there and bellow until doomsday!"

With trembling legs, Peter Jonsson climbed back up onto the sleigh.

"Run, Rose, run! Now your master wants to go home.

"Never again will I go to town, never again!" whispered Peter Jonsson. "I will never forget this day!"

No, Peter Jonsson never forgot that day. But he had, right then, forgotten that he had just bought a little calf.

Johan shoveled until the snow flew, starting right at the front steps. Then he had to shovel a narrow path down to the road. It had stopped snowing, so this was a good time to shovel. In any case, it felt nice to attack the huge snow drifts. Johan was still full of fury and despair, and mad at God. Mom had been standing at the sink, crying, when he came home from school. Dad had gone to try to borrow money for a new cow. But for those who are poor, there are no loans. God should have seen to it that Emma didn't swallow a nail in the first place. Johan shoveled and shoveled. It was dark out, but the stars shone. Soon he would be at the road.

Then he heard it, a pitiful bellow. First he thought it was his imagination, but then he heard it again: Muuh. It was heart-wrenching.

Something moved in the ditch. He rushed over. There was a calf!

Johan stood stock-still under the stars. *It was a calf.* God had thrown down a calf from his heaven; there was no other explanation. A calf that would grow and become big and take Emma's place.

"Dear God," murmured Johan. "Thank you!"

He lifted up the calf, struggling up the path until he finally reached the kitchen. Mom was out in the hen-house, so Johan took the calf out of the sack by himself before she came back in. Just then Dad came home, too. And there stood Johan, in the middle of the kitchen, his arms around a little brown calf. His eyes sparkled.

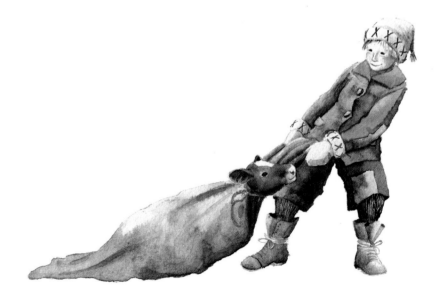

Peter Jonsson woke up the next morning and remembered that he had bought a heifer calf, but he could not figure out where she had gone.

And Johan's dad spent the whole morning trying to explain to his son that God has other things to do than sit around throwing calves down into country ditches.

"Someone owns her, you can be sure of that," he said, and patted his son worriedly on the head.

"She is mine," said Johan stubbornly. "I found her in the ditch — however she got there."

And then he went out to the barn to see the little brown calf. She stood there on her wobbly legs in her pen and bellowed softly and licked Johan's hand with her rough tongue.

But calves must have milk, and they didn't have any on the farm these days. Johan got permission to go up to Fairbrook to buy some. And Dad went along, too, because he had a vague suspicion who the calf's owner might be.

Peter Jonsson walked around his cow barn, pondering. Where could that calf have gone? Incomprehensible!

Peter Jonsson was a little ashamed — actually not just a little, for that matter. And he should be.

The door to the cow barn opened and Olson stepped in, Olson and his little boy, Johan.

Johan looked around with wide eyes. What a lot of cows. If they had just one of them at home! He knew very well that Dad was right when he said the little calf could not replace Emma. But that didn't really matter. You couldn't ask that God throw down a full-grown cow. And even if it did take a long time, the calf would eventually grow up. Right now Johan loved her so dearly just because she was small and helpless.

Dad was talking with Peter Jonsson.

"Did you, by any chance, lose a calf?" he asked.

"Have you found one?" Peter Jonsson asked cautiously.

"Not I," said Johan's dad. "But my son did. In the ditch. Is it yours?"

"Yes," said Peter Jonsson, embarrassed. "It's mine."

Johan's eyes grew wide. He stared hard at the wall. He wouldn't dream of crying in front of Peter Jonsson.

It is true that Peter Jonsson drinks now and then. And he might have other faults as well. But he is kind, no one can deny that, and he is absurdly fond of children. He saw at once that Olson's little boy was upset.

"What's the matter with this little boy?" he asked kindly.

"We lost our cow the day before yesterday," explained Johan's dad. "The boy is taking it hard."

"Oh, dear, dear me," said Peter Jonsson sympathetically. But now he had to think about the incident with the calf, which had come to haunt him. Such a misfortune! If word of this got out in the parish, everyone would say, "Peter Jonsson was so drunk that he lost his calf in a ditch." That would not sound very good. He wished that he had never bought a calf. He wished that he were rid of it and would never be reminded of his trip to town again.

Get rid of it! In Peter Jonsson's penny-pinching brain there arose an astonishing and startling thought. At first, he himself did not think he was quite sane. But the more he thought about it, the better he liked his idea.

"Johan," he said at last, "do you want the calf? You may have her."

A clear light spread across Johan's face, a clear, shining light. It is truly remarkable, thought Peter Jonsson, how children can look so happy. And it *is* wonderful when children look that happy. But then he came to his senses. He lifted his finger with great deliberation.

"On one condition," he said. "We will not utter one single word about how you got this cow! Not one word do I want to hear — remember that!"

Both Olson and Johan promised. Not one word!

Then they bought milk for the calf, and Peter Jonsson carefully counted the payment for each and every drop. He was not completely without good sense and reason.

Johan was in a hurry now. He wanted to get home to his calf. She would get her milk and then she could lick Johan as much as she wanted!

Peter Jonsson stood in the barn door and looked after them as they trudged through the snow. He tried to remember just how he did get home last night. It began to come back to him.

Peter Jonsson smiled.

"Hey, Johan," he called. "Your calf had the trip of her life last night!"